A Scholastic Australia Book

WHY WON'T YOU SLEEP?!

Adam Wallace

Carla Martell

Scholastic Australia
An imprint of Scholastic Australia Pty Limited
PO Box 579 Gosford NSW 2250
ABN 11 000 614 577
www.scholastic.com.au

Part of the Scholastic Group
Sydney • Auckland • New York • Toronto • London • Mexico City
New Delhi • Hong Kong • Buenos Aires • Puerto Rico

Published by Scholastic Australia in 2022.

To Mum, sorry for all the times I never went to sleep! – AW

For Buster, who takes AGES to get to sleep! – CM

NATIONAL LIBRARY OF AUSTRALIA

A catalogue record for this book is available from the National Library of Australia

ISBN: 978-1-76112-055-8

Typeset in Argone LC and Sugar and Spice Hands.

Printed in China by RR Donnelley.

Scholastic Australia's policy, in association with RR Donnelley, is to use papers that are renewable and made efficiently from wood grown in responsibly managed forests, so as to minimise its environmental footprint.

10 9 8 7 6 5 4 3 2 1

22 23 24 25 26 / 2

OH, HI THERE!

Can't sleep? It sure can be hard to nod off to dreamland sometimes, but I'll help you. I know *ALL* the tricks that help people sleep.

Counting sheep always works.
Look at her—isn't she cute?
OK, let's count.

ONE.

Still awake, huh?
Must need *MORE* sheep.

COUNT THESE!

Right, counting sheep does NOT always work.
I know! I'll sing you a soothing lullaby.

WEIRD . . . that should have worked. Ahhh, I know what it is. You're not tucked in properly!

Pull up your blanket.

Higher!

No, *HIGHER*!

THIS HIGH!

Are you *STILL* awake? I'm starting to get the idea you're not tired enough. Let's exercise to tire you out. Then you'll sleep for sure!

WHY WON'T YOU SLEEP?!

These are tried and true methods!

I know. I'll run you a nice, warm bath.
That's sure to make you sleepy.

What's wrong? Why won't you get in?

Oh. You want ME to test the water?

AAAGGGHHHH!

It's FREEZING! We must have run out of hot water!
I mean, it's fine once you're in.
So . . . relaxing.

But you're STILL awake!
PLEASE, GO TO SLEEP!

I have one more thing to try. How about a nice, calming *BEDTIME STORY*? I'll warm up while you choose your favourite book.

It was a dark and stormy night.
Get ready for a terrible fright!

Werewolves howl and zombies roar.
The vampire's teeth are sharper
than before!

Clouds cover the moon, rain fills the sky.
The cyclops searches with his one eye.

They're hungry, they're starving—what will they do? Perhaps they'll come and eat . . .

YOU?

ARGH! Why would anyone write a book like that?
It was terrifying! You will NEVER go to sleep now!

Go and brush your teeth. I'll wait here on your bed. Oh, your bed is rather COMFY. I might just rest my eyes . . .

ZZZZZZZZZZZZZ